W9-AVL-970

To Ivory, Jenny, and Eddie
—A. D.

For John
—C. M.

Bill Martin Jr, Ph.D., has devoted his life to the education of young children. Bill Martin Books reflect his philosophy: that children's imaginations are opened up through the play of language, the imagery of illustration, and the permanent joy of reading books.

Henry Holt and Company, Inc. / *Publishers since 1866*
115 West 18th Street / New York, New York 10011

Published in Canada by Fitzhenry & Whiteside Ltd.,
195 Allstate Parkway, Markham, Ontario L3R 4T8.

Library of Congress Cataloging-in-Publication Data
Doro, Ann. Twin pickle / Ann Doro; illustrated by Clare Mackie.
"A Bill Martin Book."
Summary: Rhyming text describes a day's activities for twins Ivory and Jenny.
[1. Twins—Fiction.   2. Stories in rhyme.]   I. Mackie, Clare, ill.   II. Title.
PZ8.3.D735Tw   1996   [E]—dc20   95-38430

ISBN 0-8050-3802-7
First Edition—1996
Printed in the United States of America on acid-free paper.∞

1   3   5   7   9   10   8   6   4   2
The artist used watercolor and gouache with black ink on watercolor paper to create the illustrations for this book.

ANN DORO

TWIN PICKLE

ILLUSTRATED BY
CLARE MACKIE

A Bill Martin Book

HENRY HOLT AND COMPANY · NEW YORK

Who is stomping on the stairs?
Who is clomping like a bear?

Who is thinking, "Do I dare?"
Ivory, of course. Or is it Jenny?

Who's meowing like a cat,
and giving Tabs a loving pat?

Who ate so much her tummy's fat?
Jenny, of course. Or is it Ivory?

Who is jumping on the bed?
Who is standing on her head?

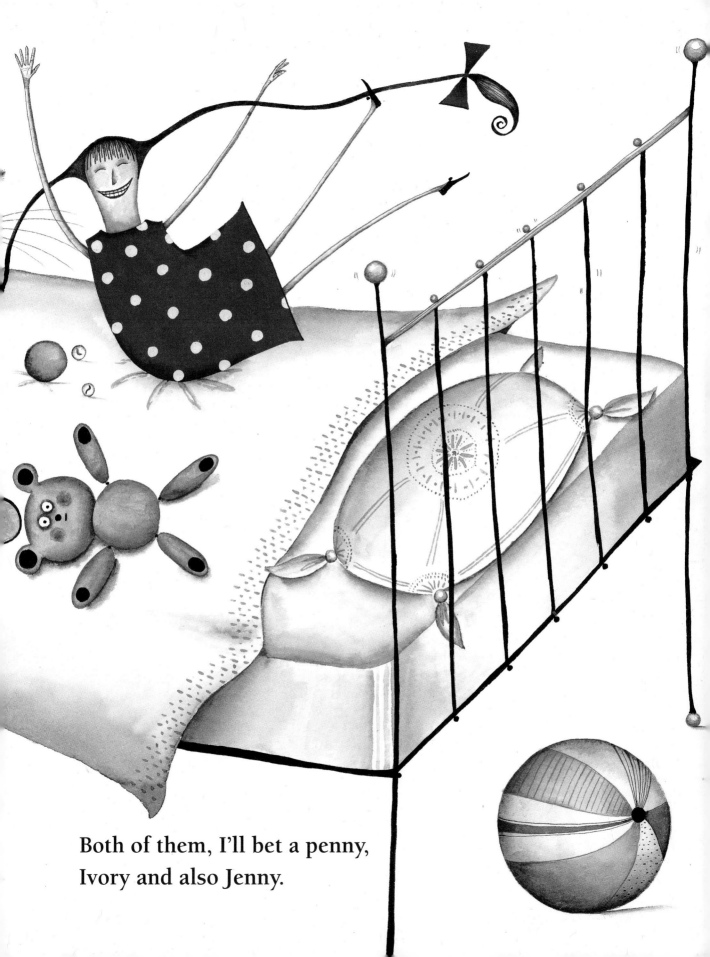

Both of them, I'll bet a penny,
Ivory and also Jenny.

Who's all dressed up to go to town?
Who is wearing a purple gown?

Who wishes she could wear a crown?
Jenny, of course. Or is it Ivory?

Who is wearing an impish grin?
Who will not tell me where she's been?

What mischief has that girl been in?
Ivory, of course. Or is it Jenny?

Who is twirling round and round?
And who needs to get unwound?

Both of them, it's plain to see,
Jenny and, of course, Ivory.

Who is stretching up so tall?
Who is bouncing that big ball?

Who left mud prints on the wall?
Ivory, of course. Or is it Jenny?

Who is learning how to sew?
Who feeds the chicks to help them grow?

Who's planting seeds in a neat row?
Jenny, of course. Or is it Ivory?

Who's pestering her brother, Eddie?
Who's cuddling a bear named Teddy?

At dinnertime, who's never ready?
Ivory and her twin, Jenny.

Who is sitting on Daddy's lap,
and wearing his big baseball cap?

Who's helping Daddy read a map?
Jenny, of course. Or is it Ivory?

Who likes to brush her grandma's hair,
or hide behind her great big chair

and tell her that she isn't there?
Ivory, of course. Or is it Jenny?

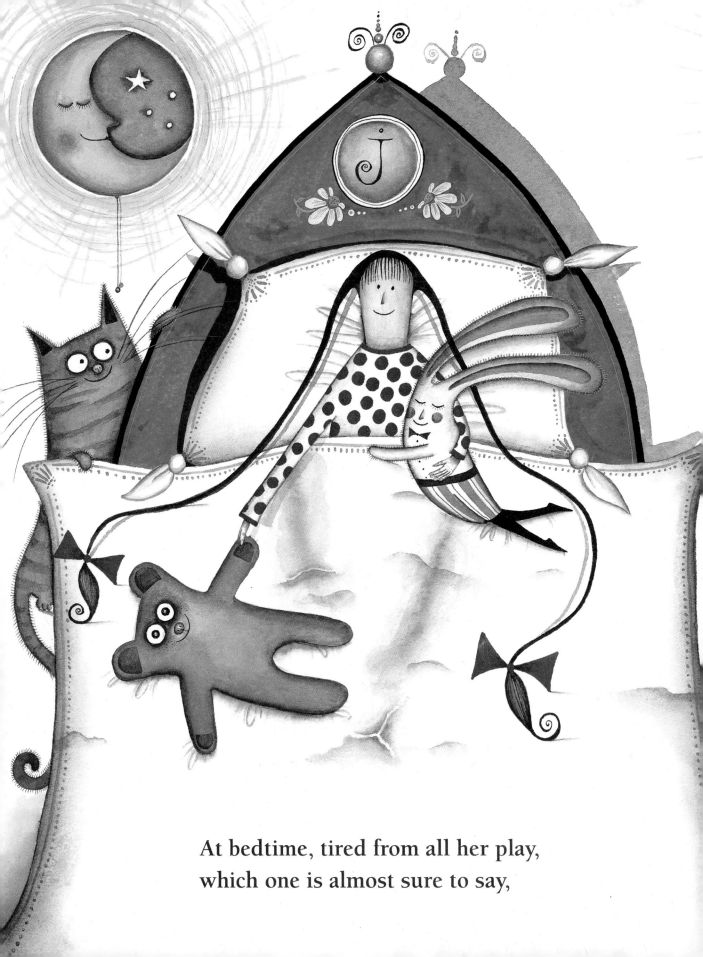

At bedtime, tired from all her play,
which one is almost sure to say,

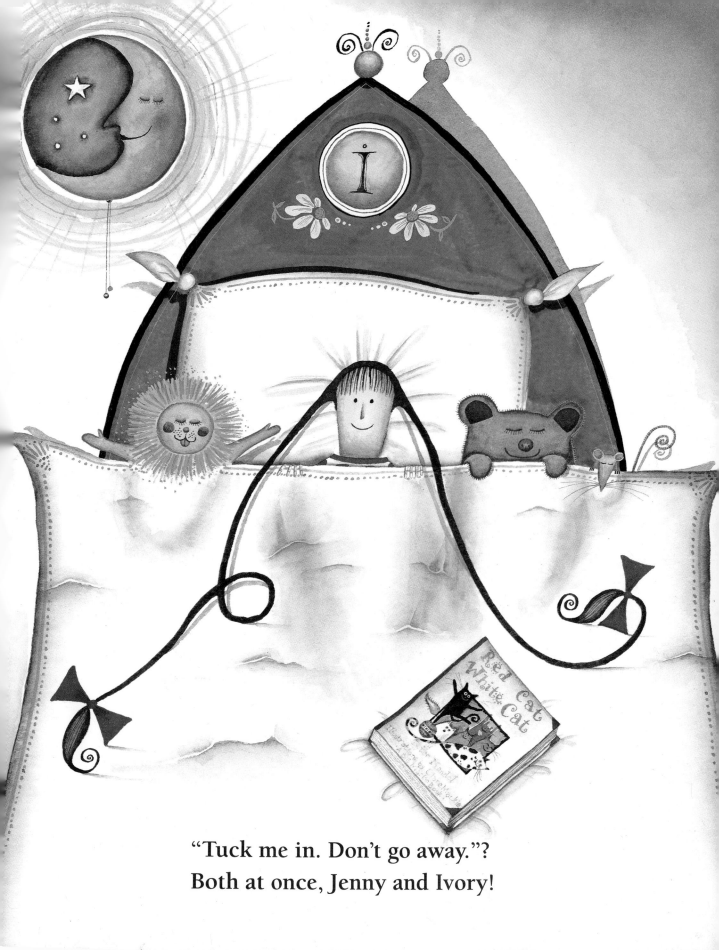

"Tuck me in. Don't go away."?
Both at once, Jenny and Ivory!